AVIGNON

MADELINE AND THE GYPSIES

Also by Ludwig Bemelmans

2

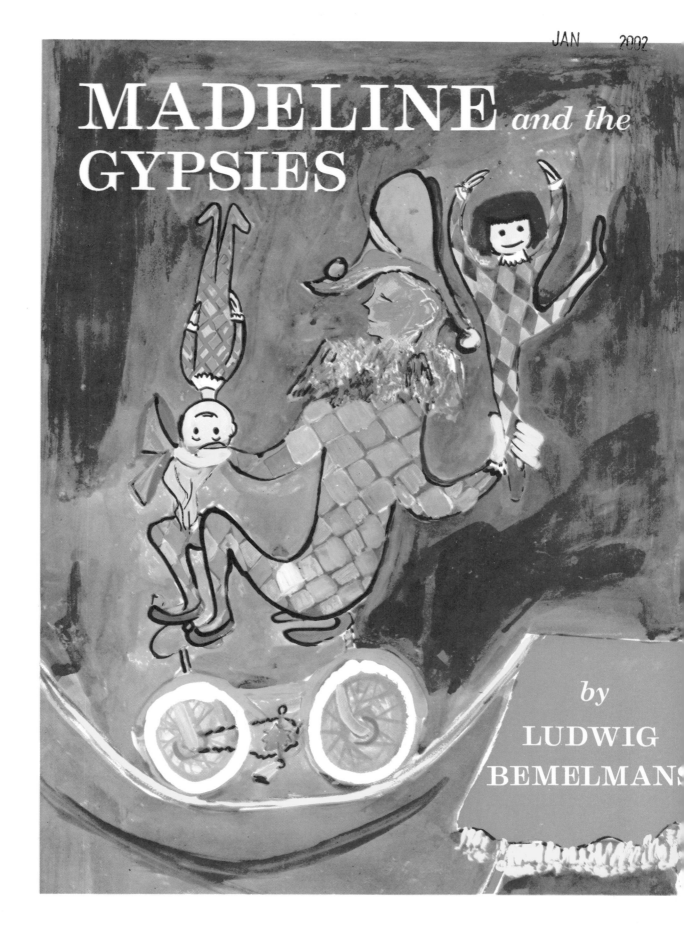

MADELINE *and the* GYPSIES

by
LUDWIG BEMELMANS

VIKING · NEW YORK

VIKING

A Division of Penguin Books USA Inc., 375 Hudson Street, New York, New York 10014
Penguin Books Ltd, 27 Wrights Lane, London W8 5TZ (Publishing & Editorial), and
Harmondsworth, Middlesex, England (Distribution & Warehouse)
Penguin Books Australia Ltd, Ringwood, Victoria, Australia
Penguin Books Canada Ltd, 10 Alcorn Avenue, Toronto, Ontario, Canada M4V 3B2
Penguin Books (N.Z.) Ltd, 182–190 Wairau Road, Auckland 10, New Zealand

Copyright © Ludwig Bemelmans, 1958, 1959
Copyright © renewed Madeleine Bemelmans and Barbara Bemelmans, 1986, 1987
All rights reserved
First published in 1959 by The Viking Press, Inc.
Published simultaneously in Canada
A shorter version of this story appeared in *McCall's*
Printed in Hong Kong
ISBN 0-670-44682-3

28 30 29

In an old house in Paris that was covered with vines
Lived twelve little girls in two straight lines.
In two straight lines they broke their bread
And brushed their teeth and went to bed.
They left the house at half-past nine—
The smallest one was Madeline.
In another old house that stood next door
Lived the son of the Spanish Ambassador.
He was all alone; his parents were away;
He had no one with whom to play.
He asked, "Please come, I invite you all,
To a wonderful Gypsy Carnival."
And so—
Dear reader—

Here we go!

Up and down and down and up—
They hoped the wheel would never stop.
Round and round; the children cried,
"Dear Miss Clavel, just one more ride!"

A sudden gust of wind,
A bolt of lightning,

Even the Rooster found it frightening.

The big wheel stops; the passengers land.

How fortunate there is a taxi stand!

"Hurry, children, off with these things!
You'll eat in bed."
Mrs. Murphy brings
The soup of the evening; it is half-past nine.

"Good heavens, where is MADELINE?"

Poor Miss Clavel, how would she feel
If she knew that on top of the Ferris wheel,
In weather that turned from bad to rotten,
Pepito and Madeline had been forgotten?

Pepito said, "Don't be afraid.
I will climb down and get some aid."
It was downpouring more and more
As he knocked on the Gypsies' caravan door.

The Gypsy Mama with her umbrella went
And got some help in the circus tent.
With the aid of the strong man and the clown,
Madeline was safely taken down.

The Gypsy Mama tucked them in
And gave them potent medicine.

The big wheel was folded, and the tent.
They packed their wagons and away they went.
For Gypsies do not like to stay—
They only come to go away.

A bright new day—the sky is blue;
The storm is gone; the world is new.

This is the Castle of Fountainblue—
"All this, dear children, belongs to you."

How wonderful to float in a pool,
Watch other children go to school,

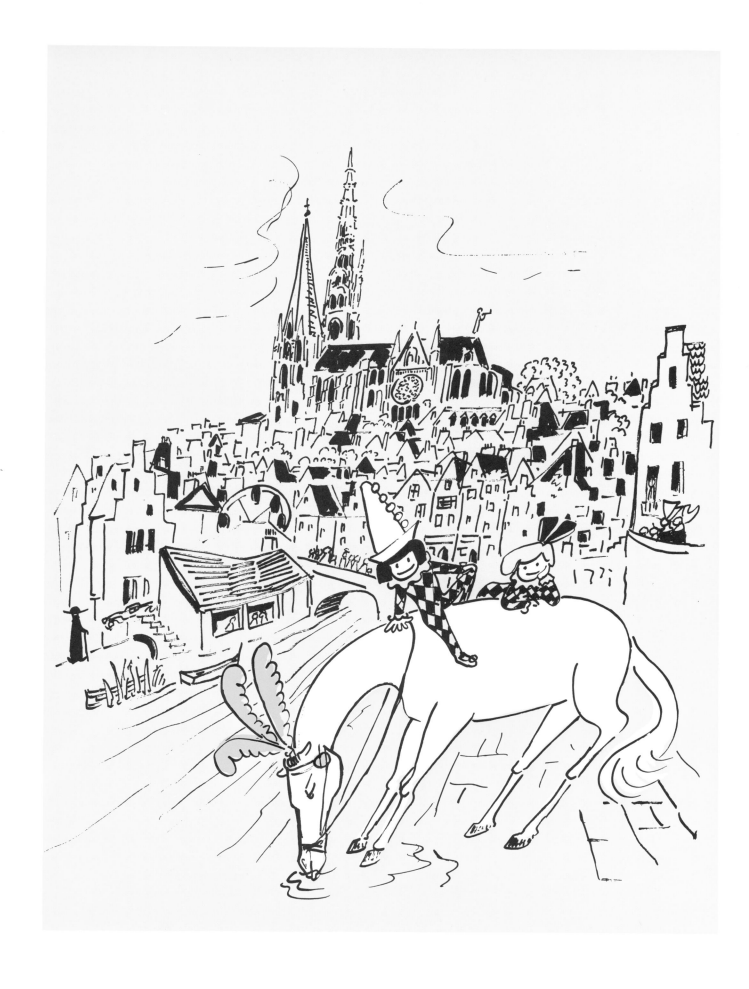

Never to have to brush your teeth,

And never—never—

To go to sleep.

The Gypsies taught them grace

And speed,

And how to ride

The circus steed.

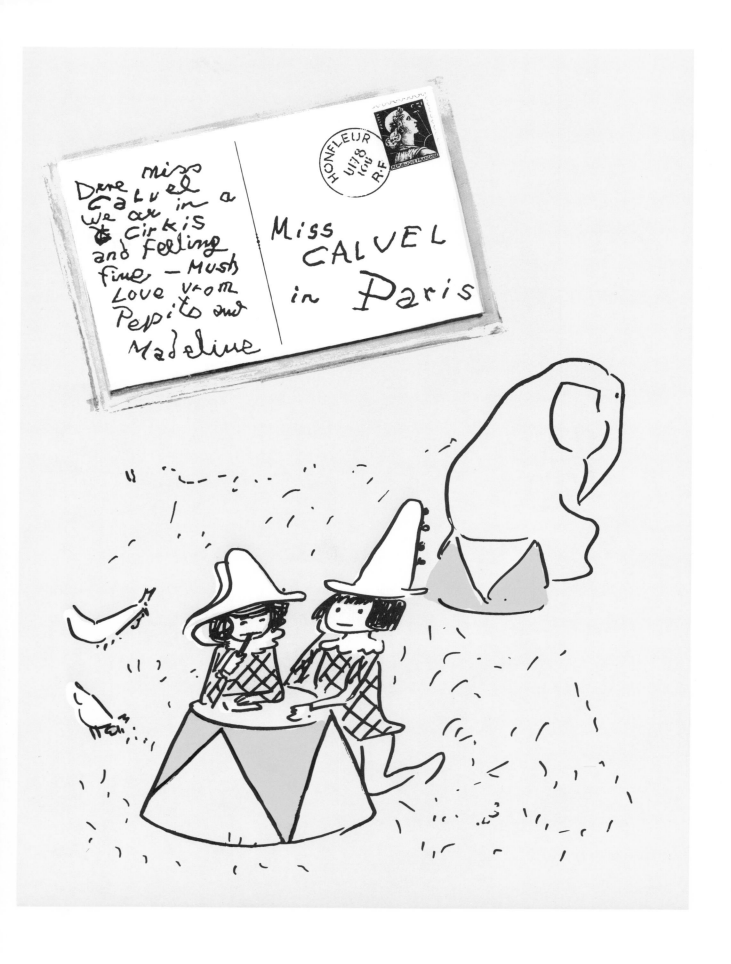

Then Madeline said, "It's about time
We sent dear Miss Clavel a line."

Poor Miss Clavel—a shadow of her former self
From worrying, because, instead of twelve,
There were only eleven little girls—
Stopped brushing their curls
        And suddenly revived
        When the postal card arrived.
"Thank heaven," she said, "the children are well!
But dear, oh dear, they've forgotten how to spell."
She studied the postmark, and then fast and faster

They rushed to the scene of the disaster.

The Gypsy Mama didn't like at all
What she saw in her magic crystal ball.

The Gypsy Mama said, "How would you like to try on
This lovely costume of a lion?"

With a curved needle and some string
She sewed both the children in,
And nobody knew what was inside
The tough old lion's leathery hide.

A circus lion earns his bread
By scaring people half to death.

And after doing that, he's fed.

And after that, he's put to bed.

A lovely dawn and all was well;

The lion roamed through wood and dell.

He smelled sweet flowers; he came to a farm;

He frightened the barnyard—

Intending no harm.

They saw a man and said, "Please help
Us to get out of this old pelt."

The man was a hunter; he took his gun;
He got to his feet and started to run.

Said the lion, "We'd better go back, for if we're not
In a zoo or circus, we'll surely be shot."

They got to the tent
In time for the show.

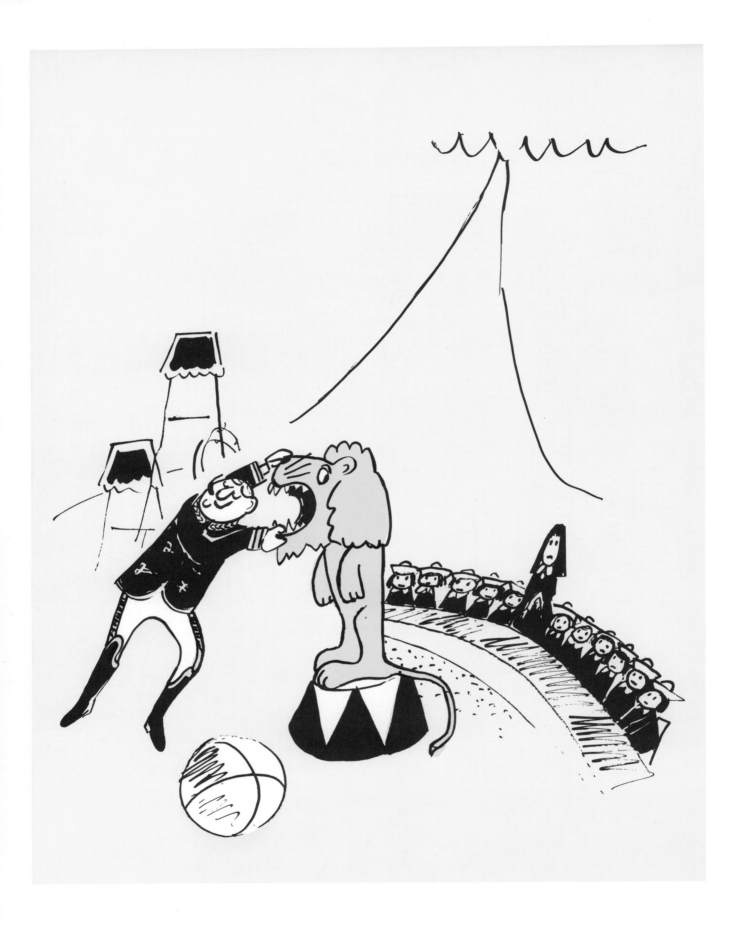

"Look," said Madeline,
"There in the first row—"

"Oh yes," said Pepito,
"There are people we know!"

"Dear Miss Clavel! at last we found you!
Please let us put our arms around you."

The Gypsy Mama sobbed her grief
Into her only handkerchief.

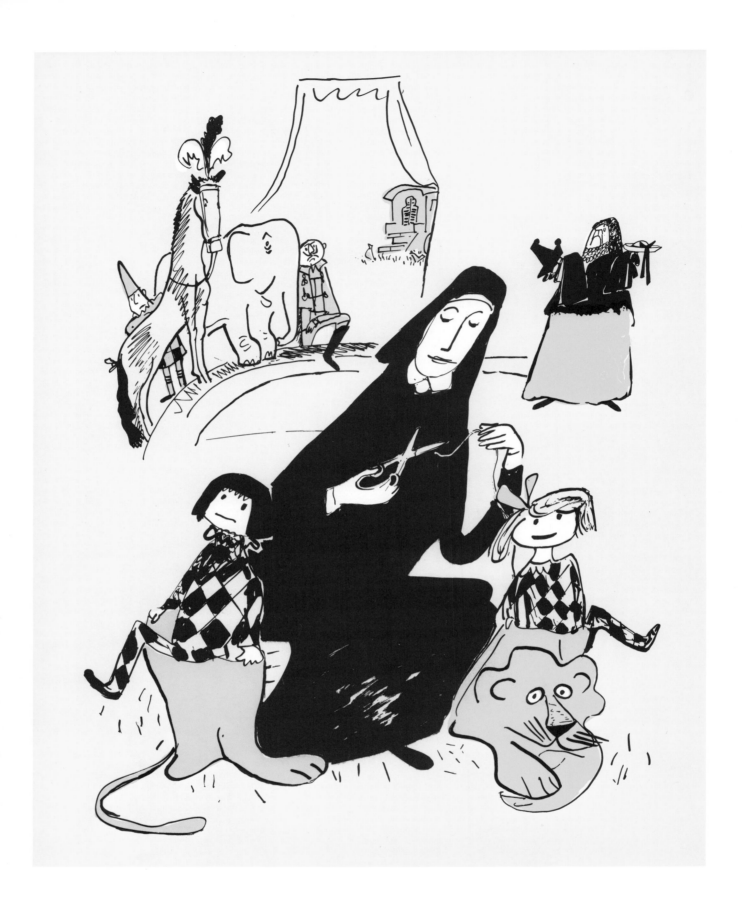

The strong man suddenly felt weak,
And tears were running down his cheek.
Even the poor clown had to cry
As the time came to say good-by.

The best part of a voyage—by plane,
By ship,

Or train—

Is when the trip is over and you are

Home again.

Here is a freshly laundered shirty—
It's better to be clean than dirty.

In two straight lines
They broke their bread
And brushed their teeth
And went to bed.

"Good night, little girls, thank the Lord you are well!
And now PLEASE go to sleep," said Miss Clavel.
And she turned out the light and closed the door—

And then she came back, just to count them once more!

Scenery in

MADELINE
and the Gypsies

LE PONT